Thank you, Mum, Dad, Brian and Colin – C R

Copyright © 2006 by Good Books, Intercourse, PA 17534
International Standard Book Number: 1-56148-510-1
Library of Congress Catalog Card Number: 2005022187

Text and illustrations copyright © Catherine Rayner 2006

Original edition published in English by Little Tiger Press,
an imprint of Magi Publications, London, England, 2006.

Printed in China

Library of Congress Cataloging-in-Publication Data

Rayner, Catherine.
Augustus and his smile / by Catherine Rayner.
p. cm.

Summary: After searching mountains, forests, oceans, and deserts to
find his smile, Augustus the tiger finds it when he looks in a puddle,
and realizes that "happiness is everywhere around him."
ISBN 1-56148-510-1 (hardcover)
[1. Happiness--Fiction. 2. Smile--Fiction. 3. Tigers--Fiction.]   I. Title.

PZ7.R2297Aug 2006
[E]--dc22
2005022187

AUGUSTUS AND HIS
SMILE

CATHERINE RAYNER

Good Books

Intercourse, PA 17534
800/762-7171
www.GoodBks.com

Augustus the tiger was sad.

He had lost his smile.

So he did a HUGE tigery stretch

and set off to find it.

First he crept
under a cluster
of bushes. He found
a small, shiny beetle,
but he couldn't see
his smile.

Then he climbed to the tops of the tallest trees.
He found birds that chirped and called,
but he couldn't find his smile.

Further and further Augustus searched.

He scaled the crests of the highest mountains where the snow clouds swirled, making frost patterns in the freezing air.

He swam to the bottom of the deepest ocean
and splished and splashed with shoals of tiny, shiny fish.

He pranced and paraded through the
largest desert, making shadow shapes
in the sun. Augustus padded further

and further

through shifting sand

until . . .

... pitter-
   patter,

     pitter-
        patter,

           drip,

              drop,

                 plop!

Augustus danced and raced as raindrops bounced and flew.

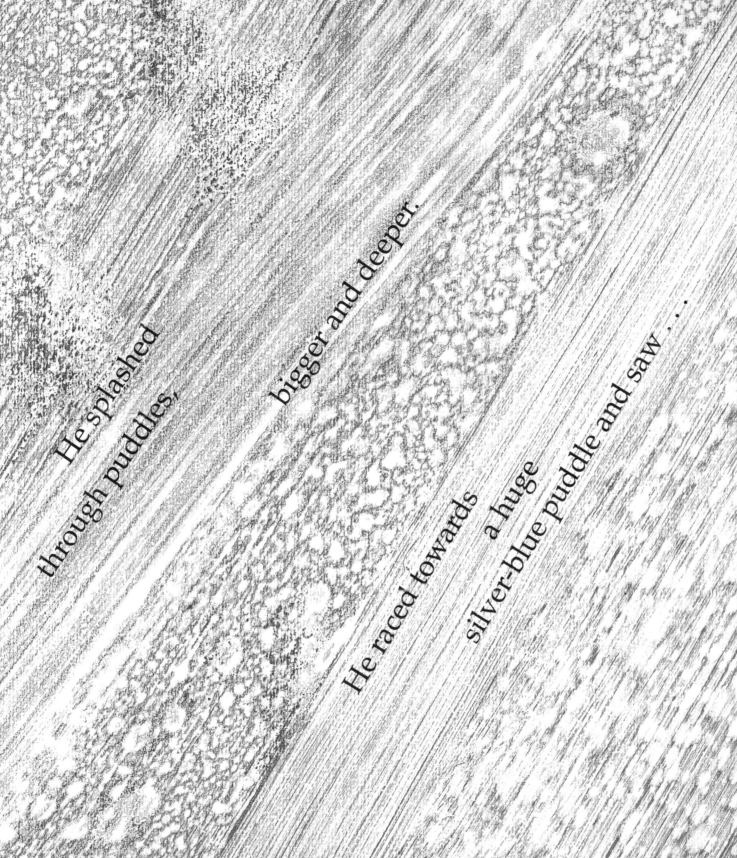

He splashed
through puddles,

bigger and deeper.

He raced towards
a huge
silver-blue puddle and saw . . .

. . . there, under his nose

. . . his smile!

And Augustus realized that his smile would be there
whenever he was happy.

He only had to swim with the fish
or dance in the puddles
or climb the mountains and look at the world –
for happiness was everywhere around him.

Augustus was so pleased that
he hopped

and skipped . . .

. . . and jumped away,
smiling.